Little Town
at the
Crossroads

Maria D. Wilkes

Illustrations by Dan Andreasen

HarperTrophy®
A Division of HarperCollinsPublishers

To my mother and father,
whose loving home I
return to again and again,
in thought, in spirit, and in heart.

Harper Trophy®, ✦®, Little House®, and The Caroline Years™
are trademarks of HarperCollins Publishers Inc.

Little Town at the Crossroads
Text copyright © 1997 by HarperCollins Publishers Inc.
Illustrations © 1997 by Dan Andreasen

Printed in the United States of America. For information address
HarperCollins Children's Books, a division of HarperCollins Publishers,
10 East 53rd Street, New York, NY 10022.
http://www.harperchildrens.com

Library of Congress Cataloging-in-Publication Data
Wilkes, Maria D.
  Little town at the crossroads / Maria D. Wilkes ; illustrations by Dan
Andreasen.
      p.   cm.
  Summary: Young Caroline Quiner, who would grow up to become
Laura Ingalls Wilder's mother, and her family have new adventures as
the frontier outpost of Brookfield, Wisconsin, grows into a bustling town.
  ISBN 0-06-440651-2 (pbk.) — ISBN 0-06-026995-2.
  ISBN 0-06-026996-0(lib. bdg.)
  1. Ingalls, Caroline Lake Quiner—Juvenile fiction. [1.Ingalls,
Caroline Lake Quiner—Fiction.   2. Wilder, Laura Ingalls, 1867–1957—
Family—Fiction.   3. Frontier and pioneer life—Wisconsin—Fiction.
4. Wisconsin—Fiction.   5. Family life—Wisconsin—Fiction.]
I. Andreasen, Dan, ill.   II. Title.
PZ7.W648389Lk   1997   96-48096
[Fic]—dc21   CIP
                                                                 AC

❖
First Harper Trophy edition, 1997.

Author's Note

Before Laura Ingalls Wilder ever penned the Little House books, she wrote to her aunt Martha Quiner Carpenter, asking her to "tell the story of those days" when she and Laura's mother, Caroline, were growing up in Brookfield, Wisconsin. Aunt Martha sent Laura a series of letters that were filled with family reminiscences and vividly described the Quiners' life back in the 1800s. These letters have served as the basis for LITTLE HOUSE IN BROOKFIELD *and* LITTLE TOWN AT THE CROSS-ROADS, *the first books in a series of stories about Caroline Quiner, who married Charles Ingalls and became Laura's beloved Ma.*

The Caroline Quiner Ingalls whom I've come to know through Aunt Martha's letters, personal accounts, and my own research is, I was surprised and delighted to discover, even more animated, engaging, and outspoken than the fictional Caroline whom millions of readers have grown to know and love. I have presented the most realistic account possible of Caroline Quiner's life in LITTLE TOWN

AT THE CROSSROADS, *while still remaining true to the familiar depiction of Ma in the Little House books. I would like to thank everyone who contributed historical and biographical information and who directed me toward significant original sources, diaries, and documents, especially William Anderson, Martin Perkins, Lorraine Schenian, Terry Biwer Becker, Cindy Arbiture, Bob Costello, and Professor Rodney O. Davis.*

—M.D.W.